Jataka Tales

Edited by Nancy DeRoin
with original
Drawings by Ellen Lanyon

HOUGHTON MIFFLIN COMPANY BOSTON 1975

Library of Congress Cataloging in Publication Data

Jatakas. English. Selections. 1975.
  Jataka tales.

  SUMMARY: Retells thirty of the five hundred tales
told by the Buddha some five hundred years before the
Christian era.
  1. Jatakas. [1. Jatakas. 2. Folklore—India]
I. DeRoin, Nancy. II. Lanyon, Ellen, ill.
III. Title.
BQ1462.E5D47   294.3'82   74-20981
ISBN 0-395-20281-7

To the Venerable Gyomay M. Kubose

Contents

Preface

The Jataka Tales are among the most famous folk stories in the world. Although little known in America, they have been read for over 2,000 years in other parts of the world and are attributed to Buddha himself, the founder of one of the world's five major religions. When Gautama Buddha lived and taught in northeast India between 563 and 483 B.C., there was no written common language. So the stories were memorized and handed down from generation to generation by word of mouth. Scenes from some were carved in ancient Buddhist sculptures and can be seen in India today.

Several hundred years after Buddha's death, the stories were written down in the Pali language. Not until late in the nineteenth century were they translated into English.

In their early written form, the Jataka Tales were "birth stories," so called because they were supposedly stories remembered by Buddha from his past lives. But belief in reincarnation is a Hindu, not a Buddhist idea. Buddha did not teach reincarnation, and Buddhists generally do not believe in it. Buddhists feel that the stories, although told by Buddha, were given their form as "birth stories" by those who wrote them down hundreds of years later.

The stories in this book were selected because they speak of issues we face today: responsibility, honesty, popularity, friendship, ingenuity, ecology, respect for the old, independent thinking, and so on. Although the language of the stories has been updated, the casts of characters and plots remain the same. The creatures and their adventures, the humor, and the wisdom are true to the originals.

The Venerable Gyomay M. Kubose, Buddhist priest, scholar, and author, has most kindly read the tales in this collection and served as consultant.

The Jataka Tales represent a branch of the same cultural root that produced Aesop's "Fables" in the West, and, as such, they provide another link with our Indo-European heritage.

The Oldest of the Three

Once, under a great banyan tree that grew on the slopes of the Himalayas, there lived three good friends—a partridge, a monkey, and an elephant.

But as time went by, their lives grew topsy-turvy. There was no order to anything they did, and they began to treat each other without kindness or respect. The partridge got up at 6 A.M., and this awakened the monkey, who usually slept all day. The monkey grumbled, and this annoyed the elephant, who stayed up late and was taking a nap. The partridge ate breakfast, while the monkey ate dinner, and the elephant ate lunch. And when the elephant wanted someone to talk to, the partridge was too tired and the monkey too cross.

Their friendship was reduced to constant quarreling. They soon found their daily lives very unpleasant. One day, the idea came to them that what they really needed was an elder who could direct them wisely.

They decided to find out who among them was the oldest and to honor that one as their leader. But how could they be sure? They had always lived together—or so it seemed—under the tree.

Said the partridge and the monkey to the elephant, "Friend elephant, how big was this banyan tree when you first remember it?"

The elephant answered, "When I was a baby, this banyan tree was only a little bush. I used to walk over it, and its topmost branches just tickled my belly. I've known this tree since it was a sapling."

Then the elephant and the partridge asked the monkey, "Friend monkey, how big was this banyan tree when you first remember it?"

"My friends," the monkey said, "when I was a youngster, I could sit on the ground, bend down, and nibble the topmost leaves of this banyan tree. I've known this tree since it was a sprig!"

The elephant and the monkey turned to the partridge and asked, "Friend partridge, how big was this banyan tree when you first remember it?"

"Friends," said the partridge, "long ago there grew another great banyan tree far from here. I used to eat the fruits of that great tree. It

1

was I who carried seeds to this spot and left them here in my droppings. From one of those seeds, this great tree grew. I knew this tree before it was born!"

The monkey and the elephant agreed. "Friend, you are the oldest of the three of us. From this time on, we will honor and respect you. And you must instruct us wisely."

And the lives of the partridge, the monkey, and the elephant were soon restored to order and harmony. Sang the three:

> The sun gets up each morning
> (And the sun is free),
> It goes to bed each night,
> Why not we?
>
> The clouds, the rain, the earth,
> This very banyan tree,
> Obey the laws of nature.
> So do we!

Sweet Tooth

When Brahmadatta was King of Benares, he had a gardener named Sanjaya. Sanjaya was wise in the ways of plants, animals, and people. One day, Sanjaya noticed a Wind Antelope—the most timid of wild creatures—near the King's park. At the sound of Sanjaya, the animal ran away. The gardener stood very still and let the antelope go without terrifying it further.

A few days later, the antelope came back. Soon, it began to roam about the edges of the park, feeding on the grass that grew there.

The king was looking out of his palace window one day and noticed the antelope near the park. He called for Sanjaya and said:

"Have you noticed anything strange near the park, friend gardener?"

"Only a Wind Antelolpe that has been grazing there, sir," Sanjaya answered.

"A Wind Antelope!" the king exclaimed. "No one has ever captured a Wind Antelope alive. Do you think you could catch this one?" he asked.

"Only give me a little honey, and I'll bring the animal right into your majesty's palace," Sanjaya answered.

Surprised and very curious, the king ordered the honey to be given to the gardener.

Sanjaya took some of the honey to the place where the Wind Antelope roamed and spread it on the grass. Then he hid himself. Before long, the antelope came. It tasted the honey carefully at first but soon began to eat with pleasure. The antelope was so pleased with the taste of honey that it started coming back to the park each day to feed. And each day the gardener spread the grass with honey, and the Wind Antelope ate its fill.

After a while, Sanjaya began to show himself. The first time, the antelope rushed wildly away. But, lured by the taste of honey, it came back again. Soon, it no longer ran from the sight of the gardener.

Sanjaya saw that the creature was addicted to honey, and the gardener knew he could now make good his promise to the king. The next day, when the antelope came, Sanjaya was waiting.

4

The gardener had a gourd full of honey strapped to his shoulder and a bunch of grass stuffed into his belt. He walked ahead of the antelope, dropping a trail of honey grass behind him as he went. The antelope followed the trail of grass, eating—until at last it found itself inside the palace. The doors slammed shut; the Wind Antelope was caught!

At the sight of the king and his men, the antelope dashed about the palace hall in fear and trembling. The king pointed to the terrified animal and said:

"The Wind Antelope is said to be so timid that for a whole week it will not revisit a spot where it has seen a human. Once it has been badly frightened, it will never return to that place again in all its life. Yet, craving for honey has trapped this wild thing. Truly, my friends, there is nothing worse than craving!"

Sanjaya said:

> Once addicted to a taste,
> Man or beast is never free;
> Not spear, or trap, or net, but taste
> Captured this wild thing for me.

After these words, the king opened the doors and let the Wind Antelope return to the freedom of its forest home.

Fearing the Wind

Once upon a time in the forest near Benares, a beautiful young elephant lived. She was as white as crane's down, and her size, strength, and height were so great that she was captured for the king.

The king entrusted this elephant to his elephant trainers to be taught to stand firm and to follow commands. The trainers tied the young elephant to a stake. Each time she could not obey an order, they beat her or poked her with an elephant goad. Maddened by pain one day, the young elephant broke loose. The trainers were so frightened they ran away, and the beautiful white elephant escaped to the Himalaya Mountains.

She went so far, so deep, and so high into the mountains that the king's men who were sent to recapture her came home empty-handed time after time. Soon they gave up, and she was forgotten.

Time passed, but the elephant did not forget. A breath of wind, the rustling of leaves, or the snap of a dry twig would fill her with terror. She would run off at full speed, shaking her trunk wildly from side to side. Although she was free, she might just as well have been still tied to the trainer's post. Her mind was so troubled that she often forgot to eat, and her once-strong body grew thin. She wandered up and down the mountain in a state of constant fear.

A Tree Sprite, under whose tree the poor elephant often passed, watched her with pity. One day the Sprite appeared in the fork of the tree and, before the elephant could run away, said softly:

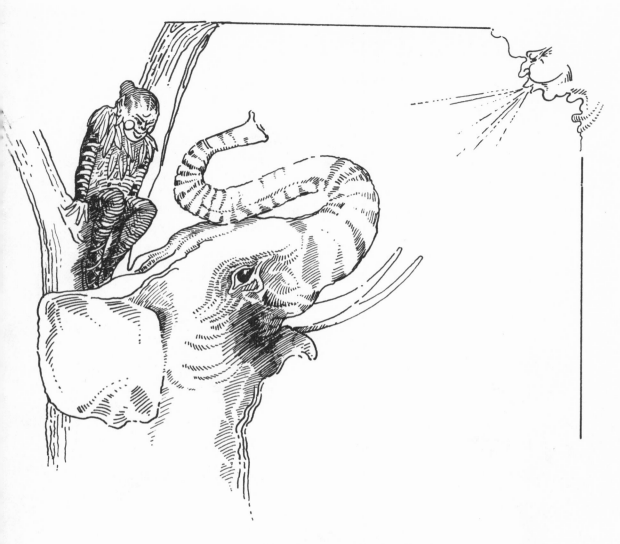

Do you fear the wind? It only
Moves the clouds and dries the dew;
You ought to look into your mind,
For fear alone has captured you.

At this, the beautiful elephant realized she had nothing to fear but the
habit of being afraid. From that day on, she began to enjoy life in her
mountain home, as she had enjoyed life in her forest home before.

The Best Food

Once upon a time in Benares on a rich farmer's estate, there lived
Big Red, a great ox, and his brother, Little Red—who was not really
little. The two oxen worked hard, plowing the fields and pulling heavy
loads for the farmer and his family. And, though they were treated
with kindness, they were fed as oxen usually are fed—on grass, hay,
and straw.

On the same farm, there lived a little pig named Munika. Munika
did no work at all, but every day he was fed dainty food—as much as
he could eat.

Seeing this, Little Red was jealous. He said to his brother one day, "Is it fair, brother, that we, who do all the work day after day, are given only grass and hay? Munika, who does no work at all, eats rice and milk. They even give him sweets! Why should he be treated so much better than we?"

Big Red, being older and wiser, said, "Don't envy anyone, brother, especially Munika."

"Why not?" Little Red asked.

But all Big Red would say was, "Wait and see."

The days went by and Munika grew fatter and fatter. The two oxen worked harder and harder, for the farmer's only daughter was going to be married, and the whole estate was preparing for the wedding.

Finally, the wedding day arrived. After the ceremony, the guests all enjoyed a great feast. The most delicious dish on the table was roast pig!

Big Red said to Little Red, "Do you see Munika, dear brother?"

Little Red hung his head and said sadly, "Yes, I see the reason now for all Munika's fine dinners. Our food, though it is grass and straw, is a thousand times better. It keeps us healthy and, best of all, it keeps us alive!"

Big Red said:

> As long as it is wholesome,
> Be grateful for the food they give.
> Poor Munika ate to die;
> Be content—we eat to live.

The Tortoise Who Talked Too Much

Long ago, one of the kings of Benares was a chatterbox. He could *not* keep quiet. Once he started to talk, no one else could get a word in edgewise. His counselors all were worried, but none knew how to put a stop to his talking, for it was not very safe to tell the king to shut up.

One day when this king and his counselors were walking in the palace courtyard, they found a tortoise lying on its back. The poor creature's shell was cracked, and he had died. The king wondered how this could have happened. The king's favorite counselor, who had been waiting for just such a chance, said:

"This tortoise used to live in a pond near the foot of the Himalayas. Two wild young geese, flying far from their home in search of food, landed on the pond. There they met the tortoise and struck up a friendship. By and by, the three animals became the best of friends.

"The day came when the two geese felt ready to fly back home. Unwilling to leave their friend, they said:

"'We have a lovely home on Mount Cittakuta in a cave of gold. Will you come home with us, friend?'

"'Gladly,' the tortoise said, 'but how shall I ever get there? If I follow you, it will take forever!'

"'Oh, it will be no problem to take you there, provided you can keep your mouth shut and not say a word on the way.'

"'That is easy enough,' the tortoise said. 'Take me with you.'

"So the two geese gave the tortoise a stick to hold between his teeth. Each goose took hold of one end of the stick and sprang into the air, flying for home. The tortoise held fast, his teeth clamped tightly on the stick.

"As they flew above the town, some village children looked up and saw this strange threesome in the air. They pointed, laughed, and jeered, saying:

"'Look at that, will you! Two geese carrying a tortoise on a stick!'

"Just as the geese were flying over the palace of the king, the tortoise felt obliged to answer them:

"'Well, and what of it? If my friends carry me through the air, what is that to you, you good-for-nothings?' But the moment he opened his mouth to speak, the tortoise fell into the king's open courtyard and split in two."

The counselor stopped speaking; then he added, "Whoever cannot restrain his own speech will come to trouble, sooner or later:

"Although his life depended on
  The stick he held between his teeth,
  The tortoise could not hold his tongue;
  He spoke—and here he lies beneath.
  He spoke unwisely, out of season;
  To his death the tortoise fell;
  He talked too much—that was the reason."

"He is talking about *me!*" the king thought suddenly. And from that day on, the king understood that there were times to speak and times to hold his tongue. He became known as a man of few words.

The Brave Beetle

Once upon a time, travelers between the lands of Anga and Magadha used to spend the night at an inn on the border of the two kingdoms. There they ate and drank and slept, and early in the morning they yoked their carts and went on their way.

One day, a dung beetle came crawling by the inn and saw a pot of stale beer left by one of the guests. He climbed up to the edge of the pot and fell in. Once in, he drank his fill of beer. Upon climbing out, he staggered down the river bank.

The ground by the river's edge was very soft and covered with the droppings of animals who came there to drink. While crawling drunkenly in the mud and droppings, a bit of damp ground gave way, and the beetle sank up to his knees.

"The world cannot hold my weight!" the beetle bawled out.

At that very moment a large elephant came to the river to drink. Seeing the drunken beetle covered with mud and dung, staggering and stinking, the elephant lifted his trunk in disgust and backed away.

When the beetle saw this, he thought, "That creature is afraid of me! See how he backs off. I will fight him!" So he challenged the elephant to battle:

> Let's be heroes, you and I.
> Come back, friend elephant, and fight.
> Are you afraid to try?

The elephant stopped to listen in amazement. At the end of the beetle's speech, he said:

> Your challenge I accept, brave bug,
> But the weapons *I* will choose,
> And not by foot or trunk or tusk
> Will you *this* battle lose!

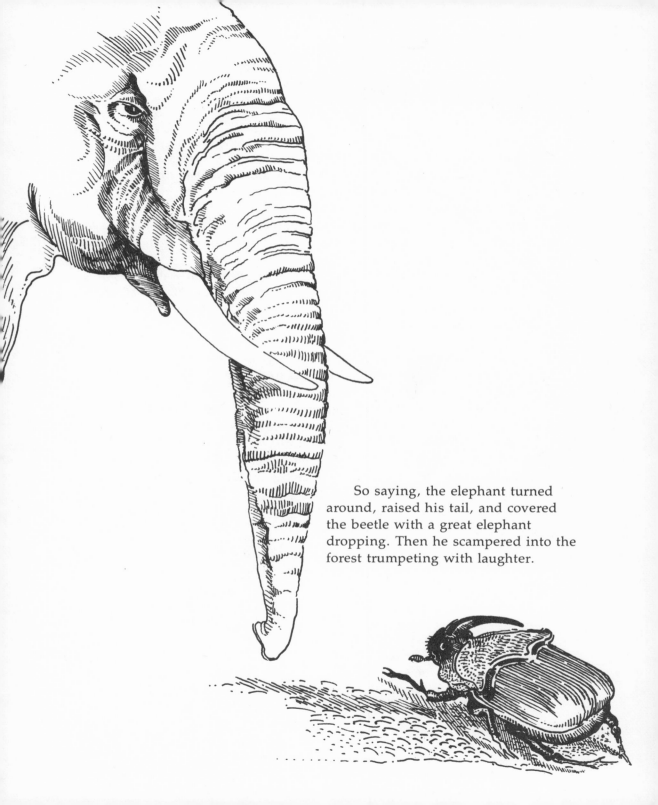

So saying, the elephant turned around, raised his tail, and covered the beetle with a great elephant dropping. Then he scampered into the forest trumpeting with laughter.

Responsibility

Once upon a time when he ruled Benares, King Vissanena proclaimed a holiday week. The king's gardener didn't want to miss any of the fun, so he called together all the monkeys that lived in the king's park and said:

"Oh, monkeys, this park is a great blessing to you. I want to take a week's holiday, but these young trees need watering. Will you water the saplings while I am away?"

"Gladly!" they agreed. So the gardener gave them watering-skins to hold and carry water, and then he left on his holiday.

In the middle of the week, the chief of the monkeys called his troop together and told them to fill the skins with water. Then he said:

"We must water the trees according to their needs. If they have long roots, they need lots of water. If they have short roots, they need just a little. You must pull up the trees to see how long their roots are before you water them."

So some of the monkeys pulled up the young trees, and others poured water on them. Of course, the sudden shock of being uprooted caused the young trees to wither and die.

The king happened to be passing by on his way to the fair, and he discovered what the monkeys were dong. He stopped and said, "Who told you to do that?"

"Why, our chief told us," the monkeys replied. The king sent for the chief of the monkeys, thinking to himself:

> If he was chosen as their chief,
> The others must be dumb beyond belief!

The monkey chief came before the king, trembling. The king demanded: "Why did you tell your troop of monkeys to pull up the young trees in the park?"

The monkey replied, "Don't be angry, Oh, king! The gardener told us to water the saplings during his holiday. If we do not know the length of their roots, how can we tell how much water to give them? Why blame us, sir, for doing our best to carry out the gardener's wishes?"

The king said to the monkey, "I do not blame you, friend, or any other creature in this park. But I do know whom to blame."

When the gardener returned from his holiday, the king showed him all the dead trees in the park. Then he said to him:

When you are made responsible,
The job is up to you,
And if you give that job to others,
You're to blame for what they do.

Blackmail

Once upon a time in the Kasi country, there lived a rich merchant who secretly buried a fortune in gold beneath his house. Years passed, and the merchant died without ever telling anyone about the secret gold. As time went by, people moved away and the village became empty.

One day, a little mouse came to live in the old house. She soon discovered the great store of gold. But since a mouse cannot use gold, she still had to hunt for her daily food. One morning as she was hurrying around the village in search of breakfast, she came upon a stone cutter digging up huge rocks near the village. She thought to herself:

"When I die, the secret of all that gold will die with me. Why not share it with this hardworking young man?" So she took a gold coin in her mouth and brought it to the stone cutter.

The stone cutter was amazed. "Why mother mouse!" he exclaimed, "have you brought this for me?"

The mouse replied, "Yes, it is for you. Perhaps you will share your food with me in return, my son."

Delighted, the stone cutter took the coin and bought a store of food for himself and shared it with the mouse. When the food was gone, the mouse brought him a second coin, then a third, and so on, day after day. The stone cutter still worked at his trade, and the mouse still lived in the old house, but both were free from hunger.

Then, one day, the little mouse was caught by a cat.

"Oh, don't kill me!" the mouse cried.

"Why not?" asked the cat. "I'm as hungry as I can be, and I really must kill you in order to eat."

"Only wait," the mouse replied. "I promise to bring you meat much tastier than I am, if only you will let me go."

"Mind that you do, then," the hungry cat replied.

So when the stone cutter came that day with food, the mouse had to share it with the cat.

The next day the cat came back. "I'm hungry again, and I am going to eat you," the cat announced.

"But I fed you and you promised to let me go," the mouse said.

"Yes, but that was yesterday," said the cat, "and today is today, and I am hungry again."

The mouse promised the cat more meat and again shared what the stone cutter brought. This went on for several days.

As luck would have it, the mouse was caught by a second cat. And she had to buy her life on the same terms. Now she was sharing her daily food with two cats. She began to grow thin. Noticing this, the stone cutter brought her more food each day. Finally, a third cat caught the mouse and began to blackmail her for food. Now the mouse had to divide her food into four parts—and her own part was pitifully small.

At last, the mouse was nothing but skin and bones. Seeing how his friend looked, the stone cutter asked her if she were sick.

She told him all that had been happening.

"Why did you not tell me this before?" the stone cutter said. "But cheer up, mother, I will help you out of your troubles."

He took a block of pure crystal and polished it with great skill until it was as clear as air. One could look straight through it and not even know it was there. Then he carved out a tiny hole, just big enough for a mouse, and told his friend to crawl inside.

He said to her, "Now, when your cats come for
their supper, be sure to tease and insult them."

The mouse waited inside the crystal. Soon, one
of the cats came and, seeing nothing strange,
demanded his meat.

"Away, you stupid cat!" The little mouse cried.
"Why should I feed you? Go home and have kittens!"

The cat could not believe his ears! And since the
mouse kept insulting him, the cat finally sprang
at her. But instead of capturing the mouse, the cat
bumped up against the crystal with such a bang that
he fell backward and tumbled away. When he
regained his senses, he was so terrified to see the
mouse completely unharmed that he ran away believing
the mouse to be a demon in disguise.

Soon, the second cat arrived. "Give me my
meat, mouse," she demanded.

"Get it yourself, you lazy good-for-nothing," the
mouse answered.

"I'll show you who's lazy." The cat snarled and sprang at the mouse with her fangs bared. But instead of sinking them into the mouse, the cat's fangs broke on the hard crystal. Just like the first cat, the second cat ran away in terror, sure that the mouse was a powerful demon.

When the third cat arrived, the mouse was sleeping inside the crystal with her little head between her paws.

"Wake up and get my meat! I'm starved," the cat said.

"Why don't you bring meat for *me* today?" the mouse suggested sweetly. "I'm really rather tired."

"*Tired*?" the angry cat screamed. "You'll soon be dead!" And she sprang at the mouse—only to come up against a solid, but invisible, wall of crystal. The third cat also ran away in blind fear, and none of them ever returned.

The grateful mouse took the stone cutter to the old house and showed him the buried fortune. The two friends, mouse and stone cutter, lived there in unbroken friendship until the very end of their lives, for, as the stone cutter said:

> One good deed deserves another,
> When it comes to friends.
> But once you try to freedom buy,
> Paying never ends.

A Handfull of Peas

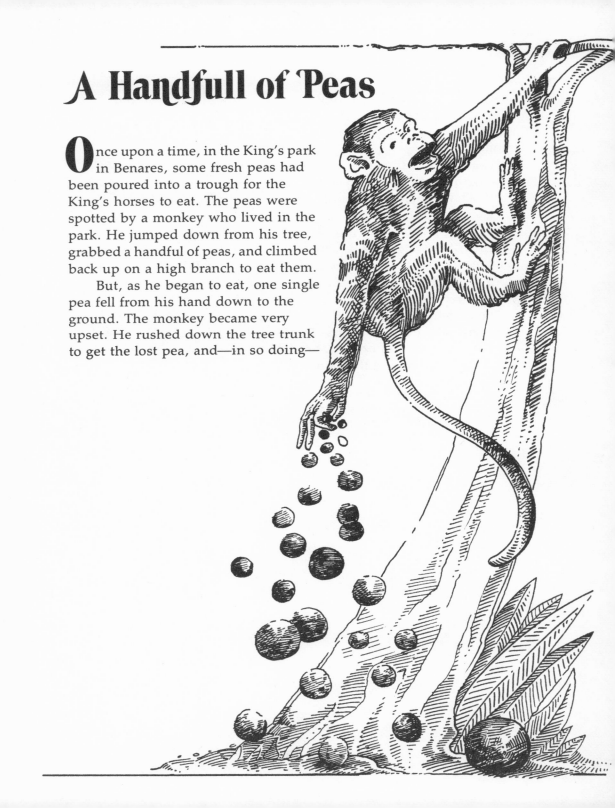

Once upon a time, in the King's park in Benares, some fresh peas had been poured into a trough for the King's horses to eat. The peas were spotted by a monkey who lived in the park. He jumped down from his tree, grabbed a handful of peas, and climbed back up on a high branch to eat them.

But, as he began to eat, one single pea fell from his hand down to the ground. The monkey became very upset. He rushed down the tree trunk to get the lost pea, and—in so doing—

he dropped all the other peas. They fell to the ground and rolled away in all directions. As hard as he looked, the monkey could not find the lost pea. He couldn't find any of the other peas, either. And since the King's horses had already eaten all of the peas set out for them, there were no more peas to be had.

The monkey climbed back onto his branch and sat there looking sad—as if he had no friend in all the world.

The King and his counselors, who had been watching the monkey all this time, laughed long and loud, until one wise old counselor remarked:

> Such are we, Oh, mighty King,
> Whenever we too greedy be:
> Risking much to gain a little—
> Like the money and the pea.

Friends and Neighbors

One day while hunting deer, a big lion slipped down a steep hill and landed in a swamp. Due to his great weight, he sank into the mud up to his neck. Try as he might, he could not get out. As soon as he lifted one foot, the other three sank in deeper. Finally, afraid to struggle any more for fear of sinking in above his head, he stood as still as a stone with only his huge head sticking out of the mud.

He stood there for seven days, his feet sunk like posts in the mud, without a bite to eat or a drop to drink.

Toward the end of the seventh day, a jackal, who was hunting for food, came upon him. Seeing a lion's head sticking out of the mud, the jackal ran away yelping in terror. But the lion called after him:

"I say, jackal. Stop! Don't run away. Here am I, caught fast in the mud. Please save me!"

The jackal came back slowly, looked at the lion, and said, "I *could* get you out I think, but I am afraid that once free you would eat me."

"Do not fear," the lion said. "If you save me, I will be your friend for life."

The jackal decided to trust him. He dug a hole around each of the lion's four feet. From these holes, he dug trenches out to the nearby pond. Water from the pond filled the trenches and ran into the holes at the lion's feet. It made the mud very soft, indeed. Then the jackal said:

"Now, make one great effort!"

The weakened lion strained every nerve, every muscle, every bone in his body. At last his feet broke lose from the mud with a loud slurp! The lion crawled onto dry land.

After washing the mud from his golden body, the great lion killed a buffalo and said to the jackal, "Help yourself, friend."

As the jackal ate, the lion noticed that he saved part of the meat.

"Why do you not eat your fill?" the lion asked.

"I am saving some to take to my mate," the jackal replied.

"I, too, have a mate," said the lion. "I will go with you."

When they neared the jackal's den, his mate almost died of fright to see a huge lion heading straight toward her cave. But the jackal called out:

"Fear nothing. This lion is my friend." And the lion said to her, "Now, my lady, from this day on I am going to share my life with you and your family." He led the jackals to the place where he lived, and they moved into a cave next to his own.

After that, the jackal and the lion would go hunting together, leaving their mates at home. Soon, cubs were born to both families, and as they grew, they played together.

But one day, quite suddenly, the lioness thought, "My mate seems very fond of those jackals. It does not seem natural to me. They are different, after all." This thought stuck firmly in her mind, and she could think of nothing else. "We are lions and they are jackals," she thought. "I must get rid of them."

So, whenever the lion and the jackal were away on the hunt, the lioness began to frighten her neighbor. The lioness would spring from hiding and snarl, "Why do you stay where you are not wanted?" Or she would creep up on the sleeping jackal and hiss in her ear, "Do you not know when your life is in danger?" Then again, she would say under her breath, "Such darling little jackal cubs. Too bad their mother does not care about their safety."

Finally, the mother jackal told her mate all that had been happening. "It is clear," she said, "that the lion must have told his wife to do this. We have been here a long time, and he is tired of us. Let us leave, or those lions will be the death of us."

Hearing this, the jackal went to the lion and said:

"Friend lion, in this world the strong will always have their way. But, I must say, even if one does not like a neighbor, it is cruel to frighten his wife and children half to death."

"Why, what are you talking about?" the lion asked in surprise.

Then the jackal told him how the lioness had been scaring his wife and cubs. The lion listened very carefully; then he called his wife before him. In front of everyone he said:

"Wife, do you remember long ago when I was out hunting and did not come back for a week? After that, I brought this jackal and his wife back with me."

"Yes, I remember very well," the lioness replied.

"Do you know why I was gone for a week?"

"No, I do not," she answered.

"I was ashamed to tell you then," the lion said, "but I will now. I was trying to catch a deer, and I jumped too far, slipped down a hill, and got stuck fast in the mud. There I stayed for a week without food or water. Then along came this jackal and saved my life. This jackal is my friend."

From that day on, the lions and jackals lived in peace and friendship. Furthermore, after their parents died, the cubs did not part. They, too, lived together in friendship, always remembering the words of the great lion:

> A friend who truly acts like one,
> Whomever he may be,
> Is my comrade and my kin,
> He is flesh and blood to me.

Using Your Head

Once upon a time in a forest near Benares, a hunter caught a large number of quail in his net. He put them in a cage, planning to fatten them and sell them at market.

The quail spent their time hopping about the cage, crying and weeping, but whenever the hunter came to feed them grain, they gobbled it greedily. Each day they ate their fill and grew fatter. But one quail did not eat. As the other birds grew fatter, he grew thinner.

The day arrived when the hunter decided to take the birds to market for sale. He took them out of the cage one by one, feeling their plump sides with satisfaction. Finally, he noticed the quail who had not eaten.

The hunter looked at the little bird in surprise. "Hello! Here's a sad looking bunch of feathers," he said. "No one would buy this bird for a cooking pot." And so saying, he took the skinny bird out of the cage and laid it in his hand to examine it.

The quail quickly spread its wings and flew away, back to the
forest, singing:

> In times of danger
> Use your head,
> Or, chances are, you'll
> Lose your head.

Harsh Words

Once upon a time in the land of Gandhara, a bull ox was born. He was given as a present to a noble Brahmin who was so pleased with the gift that he named the bull Great Joy. He treated the bull very kindly, feeding him on rice instead of hay.

Great Joy, in time, grew into a giant bull of the most amazing strength. One day he thought to himself, "This fine Brahmin has raised me with great kindness. I have had the best of everything. As a result, I am the strongest bull in all India, though none may know it. I should use my strength to repay his kindness."

He went to the Brahmin the next day and said, "Sir, find some rich merchant in town. Bet him a thousand gold pieces that none of his bulls can pull as heavy a load as I can."

The Brahmin was pleased with the idea and immediately did as Great Joy suggested. He found a merchant who had many oxen and among them many fine bulls. He said to the merchant, "Is there anyone in this town who has strong oxen?"

The merchant replied, "Oh, yes. I myself have a few strong bulls."

"None so strong as mine, I'll wager," the Brahmin boasted.

"Indeed?" the merchant said, "how many bulls do you have?"

"Only one," the Brahmin replied, "but my one bull can pull a hundred fully loaded carts."

"Impossible!" the merchant laughed. "No bull can do that."

"I'm willing to bet a thousand gold pieces on it," the Brahmin said.

"Done!" cried the merchant, and the wager was made.

The Brahmin loaded one hundred carts with sand, gravel, and stones. Then he tied them together, one behind the other. He gave Great Joy a measure of rice to eat, then harnessed him to the head cart. He himself climbed into the driver's seat and, waving the ox-goad, shouted loudly:

"Now then, you rascal! Pull them along, you great devil!"

"*Rascal*?" thought Great Joy. "*Devil*! I'm not a rascal. I'm not a devil, either!" And he planted all four feet firmly in the ground like posts and would not move an inch.

The Brahmin lost all his money and went home in an agony of grief. He was so unhappy that he went straight to bed, even though the sun was shining. Great Joy strolled to the window and looked in. He asked the Brahmin, "Are you taking a nap, Sir?"

"Taking a nap!" the Brahmin cried. "How can I possibly take a nap after I have lost a thousand pieces of gold? I will never sleep again!"

"Brahmin," said the ox, "in all the time I have lived with you, have I ever broken a pot? Or hurt anyone? Or walked in your garden? Or stepped on your children's toes? Or made a mess anywhere?"

"Never," the Brahmin said.

"Then why did you call me 'rascal' and 'devil' today? Does the thought of so much money make you forget to respect a friend and servant?"

The Brahmin was silent.

"Go back to the merchant and bet him two thousand pieces of gold. He will gladly take your bet again. But," he added, "remember not to call me names this time."

The Brahmin did as Great Joy suggested, and, sure enough, the merchant was only too glad to make another bet. The Brahmin again loaded one hundred carts with sand, gravel, and stones and tied them all together. Then he harnessed Great Joy to the head cart and got up into the driver's seat.

Waving the ox-goad, he cried, "Now then, my fine fellow! Pull them along, you Great Joy!"

The ox gave a single great pull and all the carts began to move. Soon, the last cart was on the same spot where the first cart had stood. The Brahmin collected his two thousand pieces of gold, and all the townspeople cheered the great bull.

Great Joy said,

Speak only words of kindness,
Never words unkind.
Gentle words move heavy loads,
But insults leave the carts behind.

The Dog Who Wanted to Be a Lion

Once, when Brahmadatta was king of Benares, a great lion lived in a golden den in the Himalaya Mountains.

Each day he bounded forth from his lair, looked north, west, south, and east until he spotted his prey, and then quickly made his kill. One day, he killed a large buffalo, ate his fill, and went to a clear pool to drink.

As the lion was returning to his kill, he came upon a wild dog feeding on the remains. The dog, unable to escape, threw himself at the lion's feet.

"Well?" said the lion to the dog.

"Lord of beasts," the dog said, "let me be your assistant."

"Very well," said the lion. "If you are a good assistant, you will feed on prime meat for the rest of your days."

And so the dog followed the lion to the golden den. Each day the dog would step out and look north, west, south, and east until he saw an elephant, a buffalo, a horse, or a deer. Then he would go back into the cave and report to the lion. The dog would announce in a loud, clear voice:

"Shine forth in thy might, Oh, Lord!" At this, the lion would bound out of the den and kill the beast, even if it were a bull elephant. As he had promised, the lion always shared his meal with the dog.

As time went on, the dog grew bigger and fatter. He also grew prouder and prouder. "Have I not four legs?" he asked himself. "Why am I living as a lion's attendant? From now on I will hunt elephants and other animals for myself. That lion is only able to kill them because I call out the magic words, 'Shine forth in thy might, Oh, Lord.' I'll make him call out for me, 'Shine forth in thy might, Oh, Dog.'"

The dog went to the lion and told him his wishes, saying, "Please do not deny me this."

The lion listened, then said, "Friend dog, only lions can kill elephants. The world has never seen a dog who can cope with them. Give up this foolish plan."

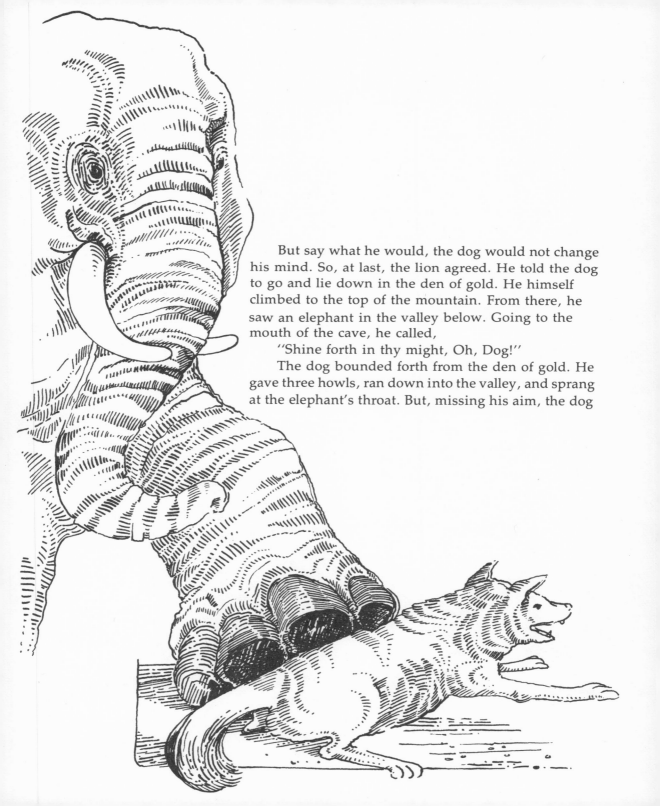

But say what he would, the dog would not change his mind. So, at last, the lion agreed. He told the dog to go and lie down in the den of gold. He himself climbed to the top of the mountain. From there, he saw an elephant in the valley below. Going to the mouth of the cave, he called,

"Shine forth in thy might, Oh, Dog!"

The dog bounded forth from the den of gold. He gave three howls, ran down into the valley, and sprang at the elephant's throat. But, missing his aim, the dog landed right under the running elephant's front feet. The enormous beast ran on, not even realizing that he had crushed the poor dog to dust.

Seeing this from the mountain, the lion said sadly:

> As a lion I was born,
> As a lion I must live,
> And as a lion die—
> There is no other way.
>
> As a wild dog you were born,
> And as a dog you would have lived,
> Had not your foolishness shone forth
> In all its might today.

Learn and Live

Once upon a time in a forest near Benares, there lived a great stag, the King of Deer. Because he was wise and clever, his herd thrived. All the young deer were brought to him by their parents to learn the ways of deer before they went into the forest on their own.

One day, the King's sister brought her first son to him and said, "Brother, please teach your nephew the ways of deer that he may live long and grow strong."

"Gladly," the King replied. Then he said to his nephew, "Kindly come tomorrow morning for your first lesson."

But the nephew did not come the next morning. Instead, he went to play in the forest. The King saw him later that day and reminded him, "Nephew, come tomorrow morning for your lesson; there are things every deer must learn in order to survive."

But still the nephew did not come. He went to play in the forest. He missed his lessons for the next five days after that. On the eighth day, as he was roaming freely in the forest, he fell into a hunter's trap. His mother, hearing that her son was trapped, rushed to the King of Deer and cried, "Oh, brother, did you teach your nephew a deer's defenses? He is caught in a trap."

The King replied sadly, "One who will not learn cannot be taught. Put him out of your mind. It is too late now."

> Although a deer has hoofs to run
> And branching antlers big as trees,
> If he won't learn to use them well,
> He might as well have none of these.

The hunter soon came and carried the young deer away.

The same mother had a second son. When he was of age, she brought him to the King of Deer and said, "Brother, this also is your nephew. Please teach him the ways of deer."

The King Deer said to the young stag, "Nephew, be so kind as to come tomorrow morning for your first lesson."

The next morning, the young stag was there before his uncle. He listened and learned quickly. Every morning for seven days the young stag came to learn the ways of deer. On the eighth day he did not appear.

His mother learned that her son was caught fast in a hunter's trap. Full of grief, she went to the King Deer, who said to her, "Have no fear. Your son has learned his lessons well:

"Six tricks my nephew knows
With which to fool his foes.

"He can," the King continued, "play dead in three positions: on his right side, on his left side, and on his back. He can go all day without water and remain strong. He can breathe from one nostril only—so softly that it looks as though he were not breathing at all. And he knows how to use his four hoofs as though they were eight. He will return shortly, I promise you."

Meanwhile, the young stag was caught fast in the trap by one leg. Using his other three legs, he pawed the ground around the trap until it looked as though a death struggle had taken place. Then he lay down on his right side and stretched all four legs out stiffly. He let his head fall backward, and his tongue hang out. He took a deep breath and rolled his eyes upward in their sockets. Then he began to breath from one nostril only. Before long, even flies and crows began to gather around, thinking the young deer was dead.

At last the hunter came to check his trap. Seeing the lifeless-looking deer and the flies and crows, he said to himself:

"This deer must have been caught early this morning, for he has been dead already quite awhile. Well, I'll carve him up right here and carry the meat home."

So saying, the hunter dragged the young stag out of the trap and turned away to unpack his hunting knives.

In a second, the deer was on his feet and, like a small cloud being blown across the sky by a strong wind, he was out of sight!

When the young stag arrived home, his mother was overjoyed, but the King of Deer was not in the least surprised to see him.

The Monkey and the Crocodile

Once upon a time, at the foot of the Himalaya Mountains, by a curve in the River Ganges, there lived a monkey. He was strong and sturdy, sleek, and very smart.

At that same time, a huge crocodile and his wife lived in the River Ganges. One day Mrs. Crocodile saw the great monkey swinging in the trees by the water's edge. "What a king of monkeys!" she exclaimed to her mate. "I can just imagine how big his heart must be. I *must* have the heart of that monkey!"

"Good wife," the crocodile protested, "I live in the water and he lives in the trees! How can I catch him?"

"By hook or by crook," she answered. "If I don't get his heart, I shall die!"

To stop her nagging, the crocodile said, "All right, don't worry. I have a plan."

So one day when the monkey came down to the bank of the Ganges to take a drink, the crocodile swam near, poked his head out of the water, and said:

"Sir Monkey, why do you eat the same old fruit day after day? On the other side of the river there is no end to the different trees, all heavy with fruit as sweet as honey."

The monkey replied, "Sir Crocodile, the Ganges is deep and wide. I cannot swim. How shall I cross it?"

"If you like, I'll carry you across on my back," the crocodile said with a wide smile that showed all his teeth.

Excited by the idea of the wonderful fruit, the monkey agreed. He climbed on the broad back of the crocodile, who swam quickly away from shore. When they reached the middle of the river where the water was deepest, the crocodile began to dive.

"Good friend, you are letting me sink!" the monkey cried. "I cannot swim a stroke!"

"Ha!" said the crocodile. "Do you think I am carrying you on my back out of kindness? Not on your life. My wife longs to eat your heart, and I am going to give it to her."

"Well," said the monkey, "it's a good thing you told me. Otherwise, you would have been very disappointed."

"Disappointed?" the crocodile said.

"Disappointed," the monkey replied. "Surely you must have noticed (clever fellow that you are) how we monkeys jump about in the trees? We go up and down, swing from branch to branch, and leap from tree to tree all the time. If we kept our hearts inside our chests, they would be knocked to pieces in no time."

"Where *do* you keep your heart, then?" the crocodile demanded.

"Why, on that tree," the monkey said, pointing back to a fig tree growing on the river bank they had just left.

The tree was heavy with bunches of ripe figs. "My heart is hanging there with all the rest," the monkey said.

"Give me your heart, and I will not drown you," the crocodile promised.

"Then take me back," the monkey replied, "and I will show you where it hangs and give it to you."

"Mind you do not pick me some other monkey's heart," the crocodile warned. "Only your heart will satisfy my wife."

"I promise," the monkey agreed. "I will not give you the heart of another monkey."

The crocodile swam back to the bank where the monkey lived, and the monkey jumped off at the foot of the tree. He climbed up the fig tree as fast as he could, sat down on a branch, and called out:

"Oh, silly crocodile! Did you really think there were animals who left their hearts hanging in trees? You are a fool, after all. Your body is huge, but you have no sense! As for your wonderful fruits on the other side of the river, eat them yourself."

And the monkey swung away through the treetops chanting:

> You say the fruits are big and sweet
> Across the river. They may be.
> No thanks! My greed for them is cured;
> It almost was the death of me.
>
> Although your body is quite big,
> Your brain, I fear, is very small;
> You are all muscle, crocodile,
> And easily outsmarted, after all!

Leave Well Enough Alone

Long ago when Brahmadatta was king of Benares, two Tree Sprites lived in neighboring trees in a great forest. In this same forest lived a huge lion and a fierce tiger.

The lion and tiger roared fearfully, scaring the village folk. And the huge beasts killed all kinds of animals to eat. They would drag the bodies under the trees to eat them and then leave the bones lying around.

One day, one Tree Sprite said to the other, "Good friend, the forest is seldom quiet because of that lion and tiger. They roar and they leave the bones of animals lying about. It looks terrible. I'm going to scare them away."

The second, and wiser, Tree Sprite replied, "True, they do roar. But that is their nature. And they do kill, but only to eat. They do leave bones lying about, but that cannot be helped. There is no perfect place on earth. You had better leave well enough alone."

The unhappy Sprite listened, but she did not understand. Day after day she brooded, moaning, "Oh, what a lovely place this forest would be if it were not for those disgusting beasts." Finally, one day, she changed herself into an awful monster as tall as a tree and appeared suddenly before the lion and tiger. In fright, the two animals ran away.

Soon, the village people no longer heard the fearful roars of the lion and tiger. Slowly but surely, they began to enter the forest. Finding nothing to fear, they began to cut down the trees.

The foolish Tree Sprite was terror-stricken. She said to the other Sprite, "Ah, this is all my fault. I could not understand when you warned me not to drive the lion and tiger away. Now that they are gone, people are clearing the forest for farm land. Soon they will cut down our trees, and we will be homeless. What is to be done?"

"Nothing," the other Sprite replied. "It is too late."

"Come back, tiger. Come back, lion," the Sprite wailed. But the two beasts were far away, living in another forest.

Before long, the people had cut down all the trees in the forest and had begun to plow the land. The two Sprites wandered over the earth in search of another home, sighing:

> Nature is hard to improve upon,
> She runs the earth, the universe;
> When we think we are making things better,
> We sometimes make them worse.

The Most Beautiful of All

Once upon a time when King Brahmadatta was ruler of Benares, two fish met head on at the place where the Ganges River and the Jumna River join.

The fish from the Ganges exclaimed, "You are beautiful!"

The fish from the Jumna cried, "You, too, are beautiful!"

The Ganges fish said, "Yes, you certainly are beautiful. But, of course, not as beautiful as I am."

The Jumma fish protested: "What do you mean? I am more beautiful than you are!" And so they fell to quarreling.

Not far from the river's edge, they saw an old tortoise sunning himself on the bank. "You, fellow," they cried, "you shall decide for us." And, swimming up close to him, they said, "Which of us is more beautiful?"

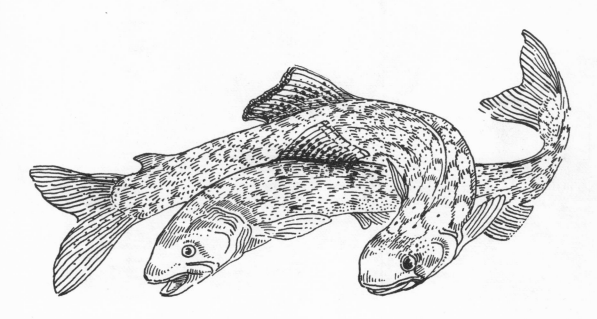

The tortoise gazed down into the water at the two vain fish and replied:

> A snake-like neck, four stubby feet,
> A round humped back, a reptile face,
> Two beady eyes and wrinkled skin—
> Now *that's* what I call grace!
>
> Since by your tongue your praise is sung,
> I feel it is my duty
> To tell you that, of all of us,
> *I* am the real beauty!

The Company You Keep

When Brahmadatta was king of Benares, he had an elephant named Damsel Face who was known for her good nature. She was strong but gentle.

One day, the elephant's keeper—an old man who had cared for her since she was a baby—fell ill. His place was taken by a young stable hand who was fond of drinking and who was a thief and a rascal as well. At night, when everyone in the palace was asleep, he let his friends into the stable. There, they would drink, swear, gamble, and quarrel until morning. They stole from the palace and from each other.

One morning when Damsel Face was led out of the stable for her exercise, she suddenly trumpeted wildly, broke loose, and scampered away. Before the eyes of the astonished king, the elephant waded into the royal lotus pond and wallowed there, pulling up lotus flowers with her trunk.

The king was sure that Damsel Face was having a fit, so he
ordered her put back in her stall.

The next day when the king was riding her, Damsel Face
suddenly ran for the nearest inn, broke into the kitchen, and sucked a
barrel of wine up into her trunk. With the king still mounted on her
back, she lurched through the town, shamelessly drunk, slapping
people with her trunk and spraying wine in all directions. It took six
men to catch her and rescue the king.

The days that followed saw the once peaceful elephant trampling
gardens, eating fruits and vegetables that belonged to hard-working
village people, and fighting with other elephants. She became bad
tempered, dangerous, and completely untrustworthy.

At last, the king decided to have her put to death. But one of his counselors said, "Sir, let me spend some time with this elephant to see if I can find out what has caused this change."

So, with the king's permission, the counselor spent that night hidden in the stable. There, he saw the young stable hand and his friends drinking, gambling, fighting, and cursing until dawn.

The next day, the counselor reported to the king. "Sir, your elephant is not sick in mind or body. She simply has been misled by bad company." And he described to the king what was going on at the stable.

"What is to be done?" the king asked.

"Get rid of the stable hand and his friends. Then let your wisest counselors work in the stable and care for Damsel Face."

People were amazed, to be sure, when they saw the kingdom's wisest men working in the stable. The counselors worked hard, were courteous to each other, and treated the animals kindly. At night, after work, they talked of honesty, wisdom, kindness, and respect.

Damsel Face once again became gentle, good-natured, and dependable.

"Well, friend," the king said to the counselor one day, "I see that Damsel Face is herself again."

The counselor replied:

> When choosing friends it's always wise,
> To look before we leap—
> Our deeds are often prompted by
> The company we keep.

Popularity

Once upon a time when Dhananjaya was king of Benares, two parrots lived in the nearby forest. One was named Radha, the other Potthapada. Both were big and perfectly formed. Their feathers were beautiful to see.

A hunter, seeking the king's favor, trapped these two birds and gave them to the king as a present.

Pleased with the beautiful birds, the king put the pair in a golden cage. They were given honey and parched corn to eat from a golden dish and sugar water to drink. The king spent a lot of time talking to them, and the parrots became the favorites of the whole court.

Then one day a forester, also seeking the favor of the king, brought a big black monkey named Kalabahu as a present.

Quickly, all the attention was turned to the big monkey. He was so comical! His funny faces made the lords and ladies laugh, and the king himself was very much amused when the monkey played the clown. No one payed any attention to the parrots anymore, although they were still fed and cared for.

The older parrot, Radha, said nothing. But the younger bird, Potthapada, complained. "Brother, in this royal house we used to get much praise. Now we get none. Lords and ladies used to give us treats to eat. Now we get only daily food. The king used to visit us and talk to us daily. Now he passes our cage without looking. And," he wept, "that monkey has all the attention that belongs to us!"

Radha said to his brother parrot, "By what right does it belong to us?"

Potthapada replied, "Because we were so good, so true, so loyal. We never bit, we never squawked. We were well behaved birds!"

"And why not?" Radha asked. "If you were being yourself, brother, you have no cause to complain. Perhaps you were just putting on an act to please the king."

Potthapada hung his head in shame.

Things continued as they were for a long while. But, at last, the monkey (who was only a foolish fellow) grew bored with his pleasant life. He even grew tired of all the good things he had to eat and drink. He became devilish and began to steal. When caught, he would put on a long face and everyone could not help but laugh.

Then, not knowing what to do next, the monkey began to amuse himself by frightening the king's children. When they came near, he would shake his ears and show his teeth. The children cried and ran away. Soon they would not enter the room for fear of the monkey. The king asked them one day why they were so afraid of Kalabahu, and the children told him how the monkey had been scaring them.

The king became angry and ordered his men to drive the monkey out of the palace and back into the forest. The parrots once again became the favorites. Potthapada sang for joy, but his brother, Radha, warned him to remember:

> Gain and loss, and praise and blame,
> Pleasure, pain, dishonor, fame,
> All come and go like wind and rain!

How Straws Were Invented

Long ago in Kosala, near the village of Nalaka-pana, a thick forest used to stand. In this forest was a lake, and in this lake there lived a water ogre who ate every creature that went into the water to drink.

In this same forest there lived an old monkey who was as big as a deer and very wise and clever. He was head of a troop of 80,000 monkeys, and he protected them all from harm. He always warned them:

"My dear friends, this is a big forest. In it there are many poisonous trees and many lakes and ponds haunted by ogres. Mind that you ask me first before you eat any fruit that you have not eaten before or drink water where you have not drunk before."

One day, the troop of monkeys came to a place in the forest where they had never been. There before them was a beautiful lake of clear, cool water. They had traveled a long way, and they were hot and almost dead from thirst. Without water they could go no farther. But rather than drink, they sat down and waited. When the head monkey arrived, he walked all around the lake. He noticed a very strange thing: all the footprints of men and animals went down to the lake, but none came up again.

"Without a doubt," he said, "this lake is haunted by an ogre that eats everyone who goes into the water to drink."

Meanwhile, the ogre who lived in the lake had seen the great troop of monkeys, and his desire to eat them overcame him. Suddenly, he appeared above the water, a horrible monster with a white belly, a blue face, and bright red hands and feet.

"What are you waiting for? Come into the lake and drink!" he bellowed.

But the head monkey asked him, "Are you not the ogre who lives in this lake?"

"I am!" the ogre said.

"And do you not eat every creature, man or beast, who goes into the lake to drink?"

"I do," the ogre roared, "and I will eat the lot of you, too!"

"No," the head monkey replied, "you will not eat *us*."

"If you do not drink," said the ogre, "you will die of thirst, anyway."

"No," the head monkey told him, "we will not die of thirst, either. Your eyes are so blinded by greed that you cannot see how easy it will be for us to drink our fill."

"How?" the ogre demanded.

"A problem has many solutions," was all the head monkey would say.

Then, while the ogre looked on, the head monkey picked one of the long, hollow water reeds that grew thickly around the lake shore. He told his troop to do the same, and each monkey did so. Then the head monkey sat down comfortably on the shore and placed one end of the hollow reed in his mouth and the other end in the lake. He sucked up the water with ease. All the monkeys did the same until they had drunk their fill.

The ogre almost burst with rage.

> "This is the very last straw!"
> The ogre cursed.
> "Oh, no," the monkey chief replied,
> "Not the last straw, but the *first*."

Trickery

When Brahmadatta ruled Benares, a fine big antelope lived nearby in the forest, feeding on fruits that fell from trees. This antelope liked the fruit of a certain Sepanni tree best and used to feed under that tree often.

About that time, a village hunter thought up a sly plan for killing antelope. Instead of tracking them on foot, he decided to ambush them where they fed. First, he planned to find fruit trees that had antelope tracks around their trunks. Finding one, he would build a platform high up in that tree. He then would climb up and, hidden by leaves, wait for the antelope to come and feed on the fallen fruit. Being directly above an antelope, he reasoned, he could kill it easily with his spear.

After searching for a few days, he found the tracks of the big antelope around the Sepanni tree. "Ah!" he said, "now I can put my plan into action." He built a platform high in the Sepanni tree, and the following morning he climed into it and waited.

Soon, the antelope appeared. He approached the tree slowly. He sniffed the wind and thought, "Something is strange here. I see no hunter, but I smell one!" And the antelope stopped some distance from the tree.

Seeing that the great antelope did not come near, the hunter grew impatient. He began to throw fruit down toward the antelope to encourage it to come closer.

"Oho!" thought the antelope. "Here's fruit coming to meet me." Then, speaking as if to the tree, the antelope said:

"My worthy tree, up until today you have been in the habit of letting your fruit fall straight down to the ground whenever it was ripe. But today you have stopped acting like a tree. And since you have stopped acting like a tree, I will stop acting like an antelope. I will not eat your fruit this morning!" And the antelope turned to leave.

The hunter, in a rage, hurled his spear down from the tree. It missed the antelope, and the hunter yelled:

"All right, begone! I've missed you this time, but I'll get you yet!"
Wheeling around, the antelope replied:

> Those who try to fool another
> Always make me laugh:
> They judge themselves twice too smart,
> The other only half!

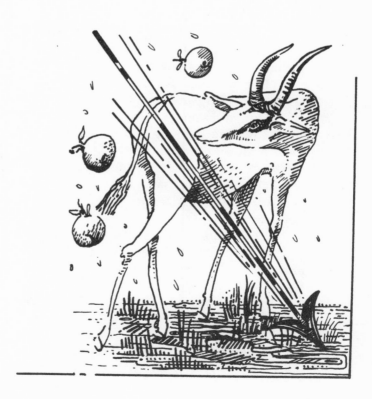

The Wonders of Palace Life

Once upon a time when Brahmadatta ruled Benares, a young monkey lived with a troop of monkeys near the Himalaya Mountains. A woodsman caught him and gave him to the king as a present.

During the winter months, the monkey lived as a palace pet. He charmed the king and the royal family with his ways. The monkey was allowed to run freely in the palace, and he learned a great deal about the ways of men.

When summer came, the king and his court prepared to move to the summer palace. The king called for the woodsman and said, "I have been very pleased with this little monkey. He has amused us very much. Here is a reward for you." And he gave the woodsman a sack of gold coins.

"Now, as a reward for this monkey, I want you to return him to the place where you captured him and set him free."

The woodsman was pleased to do as the king wished. The monkey, once free, returned to the Himalayas, and the monkey troop all gathered on a large rock to hear about his adventures.

"Friend," they asked, "where have you been all this time?"

"In the king's palace at Benares."

"How did you get free?"

"I amused the king and his court so well that the king felt kindly toward me and set me free."

"You must know all about palace life. How grand it must be! We would like to live in that grand style. Will you teach us the ways of men?"

At first the monkey refused. "No, you would not like to live that way."

But the monkeys insisted that he teach them the ways of men.

"Very well," he finally agreed. Then he picked the largest monkey and said, "Now, you are king. You must sit on this rock and order all the monkeys to bring you fruit."

The king monkey did as he was told. Each monkey brought him fruit.

"But I cannot eat all this fruit," the king monkey said.

"The fruit," said the monkey who had lived at the palace, "is not

for you to eat. It is for you to keep
in a big pile. To be king, you
must be rich. To be rich, you must
have a big pile of fruit.''

So the monkeys, wishing to
live like men, piled a mountain of
fruit behind the king monkey.''

"What next?'' they all asked.

"Now all of you must approach
the king and compliment him.''
The monkeys gladly agreed.

"Oh, King,'' one said, "your
fur is very thick and shiny.''

"Oh, King," said another, "your eyes are very bold and bright."

"Oh, King," said a third, "you are wise and very strong." And this went on until all the monkeys had spoken the king's praise.

"Now," said the monkey who had lived in the palace, "all you monkeys must go behind the king's back and say insulting things about him."

So the monkeys stood behind the king monkey and said, in turn:

"His fur is thin. I think he must be getting bald."

"His eyes are dull. I don't think his eyesight is what it used to be."

"He is as weak as a worm and almost as stupid."

Finally, the king monkey became so angry that he left his throne and started chasing the monkeys who were insulting him. When he returned, all his fruit was gone.

"My fruit! My fruit! Someone has taken all my fruit!"

"Now," said the monkey who lived in the palace, "you must find the guilty monkey and put him to death."

"To *death*?" the king monkey cried. "Oh, what are you saying?" And he covered his ears with his hands and buried his head between his knees.

"Stop! Stop!" all the monkeys cried, covering their ears. "Teach us no more about palace life." And they ran away, crying:

> Flattering, lying, stealing, killing,
> The ways of men are really chilling!
> If in a palace men do these,
> We're safer here among our trees.

How a Wolf Reforms

Once upon a time when Brahmadatta ruled Benares, a wolf lived on a rock by the banks of the Ganges River. One night while he slept, a winter flood came up and surrounded his rock. When he awoke in the morning, he found himself marooned.

The wolf thought, "I am surrounded by water. If I leave this rock, I will drown. No food here, and no way to get it. So here I sit with nothing to do until the flood waters go down. Well, this is a fine chance to think about my life. I have not always been the best of wolves. I have lived from day to day, eating and drinking, without any thought about life's true meaning. I am going to become a new wolf! I am going to reform."

Folding his front paws, the wolf said, "And I will begin by going on a fast as holy men do. I will not eat until the flood waters go down!"

Pleased with himself, the wolf lay down on the rock looking very serious and very holy, indeed.

Now Sakka, a powerful god who could change himself into any shape he wished, heard the wolf. He thought, "Let's just see how reformed our friend the wolf *really* is."

Sakka changed himself into a plump little goat and appeared on the rock. The wolf took one look at the goat and shouted, "What luck! I'll starve tomorrow!" And he sprang at the goat. Somehow the goat jumped aside. The wolf sprang again. Again the goat leaped out of the way. The wolf jumped and leaped and chased about after the goat until he was completely out of breath. Finally, he gave up and lay down. "Well," panted the wolf, "at least I have not broken my fast. I can keep my promise to reform, after all."

The goat vanished, and Sakka appeared in its place and said to the wolf with scorn:

> The wolf made a promise to reform,
> But found it hard to keep;
> The words that are hardest to live by,
> Are the easiest to speak.

The Greedy Crow

Long ago when Brahmadatta was king, the people of Benares loved birds of all kinds. They hung up baskets all over the city for the shelter and comfort of birds. The cook of the Lord High Treasurer hung a reed basket in his kitchen, and a gentle pigeon made her home there. Every morning the pigeon would leave the basket and fly away in search of food, and every evening she would return home. Thus, she lived her life and kept the cook good company.

One day a crow, flying over the kitchen, smelled the wonderful cooking smells and was filled with greed. "How can I taste some of those wonderful dishes?" he wondered. Then he saw the pigeon returning home. "Ah!" he thought, "I can make that bird my tool."

So when the pigeon flew out of the kitchen the next morning in search of food, the crow followed. Like a shadow, wherever the pigeon went, the crow was right behind. Finally, the pigeon said,

"What do you want with me, Mr. Crow? You and I don't feed alike."

"Ah, but I like you," said the crow. "I want to be your friend."

"So be it, then," said the pigeon, "but you will find it hard to eat what I eat."

The crow followed the pigeon about, pretending to eat seeds and grasses as she did. But whenever the pigeon was not looking, the greedy crow would gobble up a worm, a grasshopper, a piece of garbage—anything he could fasten his beak on. Before the pigeon had finished eating, the crow was stuffed. He said to the pigeon, "Friend, you spend too much time eating. Let us fly home." And they did.

"Why our bird has brought a friend!" the cook exclaimed when he saw the crow. And he hung up another basket in the kitchen.

The pigeon and the crow slept side by side in the kitchen that night, warm and snug in their baskets.

When morning came, the cook arrived, carrying a large plate piled high with fish to cook for dinner that night. Filled with greed, the crow lay in the bottom of his basket and began to groan.

The pigeon said to him, "Come along, old fellow—breakfast time!"

"Oh, you fly off without me, friend," the crow said. "I have a terrible stomach ache."

"A crow with a stomach ache?" the pigeon exclaimed. "Nonsense! I have never heard of a crow

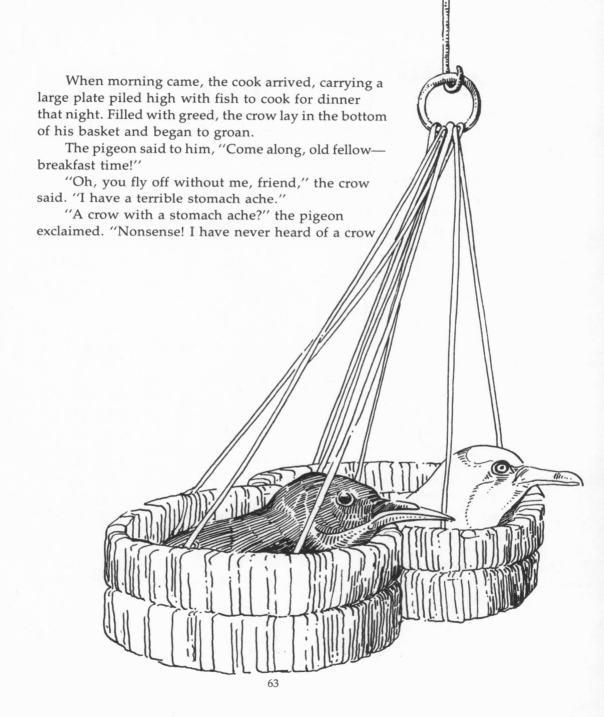

with a stomach ache. Crows can eat candles and string without getting stomach aches. Come along, I say, and don't let the sight of that fish make you greedy."

"Why, madam, what are you saying! The very idea! I tell you I am dying of pain!"

"Very well," the pigeon said, "stay home. But be sure you don't give way to greed. Our cook is kind, but not to thieves." And the pigeon flew away in search of her food.

Meanwhile, the cook began to fix the food for the day. First he mixed and baked all kinds of breads and cakes. Then he peeled and cut all kinds of fruits and vegetables. The crow lay in his basket half maddened by the wonderful smells. Finally, the cook began to spice and cook the huge platter of fish. Some he boiled in a pot, some he roasted in the oven, and some he chopped. When all the fish was put on the stove, the cook tilted the lids of his pots to let the steam escape. Then he went outside to rest and wipe the sweat from his brow.

No sooner was the cook outside the door than the crow's head popped out of his basket. His groaning stopped. "Now or never!" he thought. "The only question is, shall I have a bit of chopped fish first, or shall I have a large piece of boiled fish?" Being extremely greedy, the crow decided that it would take too long to eat his fill of chopped fish, so he flew over quickly and landed on top of the pot of boiled fish. But as he landed, his claws made a sharp "click."

"What can that be?" said the cook, running into the kitchen just in time to see the crow dip his head into the pot and come up with a piece of fish.

"Oh, that thieving crow!" the cook exclaimed. And he grabbed the crow, plucked his feathers, and threw the bird and his basket out the door.

When the pigeon returned home that night, she saw the crow plucked and unable to fly, sitting in his basket in the yard. She said to him:

"Who are you, friend, bald with old age, sitting in my friend's basket? You had better fly away, for I am afraid my friend the crow will be very angry if he finds you here!"

"Ah!" said the crow, "well you may laugh at such a sorry sight. I would not do as you told me, and now I am as bald as an egg."

The pigeon said:

I hope you sprout some wisdom, crow,
With your new feathers as they grow;
From troubles you will not be freed
Until you can outgrow your greed.

'Don't Try the Same Trick Twice

Once upon a time near Benares, a little red monkey discovered a cave in the mountains sheltered from the wind and rain, and he made his home there.

Soon, the rainy season came, and the rains poured down. One day, after it had been raining for seven days without stopping, an old black monkey wandered by. He was wet to the skin and shivering with cold. He saw the little monkey sitting in the mouth of his cave, high and dry, and wondered: "Will he take pity on an old fellow and invite me to share his cave?"

But the little red monkey pretended not to see him. The black monkey thought, "Well, there's more than one way to get inside." Puffing out his belly as though he had just eaten a big meal, the black monkey stepped up to the mouth of the cave and said:

> The figs are ripe, the banyans good,
> At the secret place I found;
> Why don't you go and eat your fill
> At that wonderful feeding ground?

And he gave the little red monkey directions to the "feeding ground."

The little monkey set off in the direction he was told, his mouth watering for some of the wonderful fruit. He searched and searched, but he could find no such fruit and no such feeding ground.

When he came back to his cave and saw the black monkey sitting inside, high and dry, he realized that he had been tricked. So he stood in front of the black monkey and patted his stomach and said:

> Happy is he who honor pays
> To his elders full of days;
> Just as happy as I now feel
> After such a tasty meal!

The old monkey listened to him, then replied:

> You left me standing in the rain,
> And now you "honor" me? Perhaps.
> But this old bird cannot be caught
> In one of his own traps!

So the little red monkey went off in search of another cave.

King of His Turf

In the time of King Brahmadatta, a young quail was born near
Benares. He lived near farms and found his food among the clods
of earth turned up by the farmers' plows. Some of these clods were
as large as boulders. When the fields were freshly plowed, the clods were
soft; but when the sun baked them, the clods became as hard as stone.

One day, the young quail grew tired of picking grass and seeds
out of the big clods of earth. He thought to himself, "I will leave
this place. Finding food is too hard here. I have heard that near the edge of
the forest sweet grasses grow and drop their seeds on flat ground. There
is no need to hop about and scratch for food." So he flew off until
he came to the edge of the forest. There, he found what he was looking
for and began to eat his fill.

But as the quail was eating, he was spotted by a falcon who lived
in the forest. Without wasting a second, the falcon attacked. He caught
the little quail in his claws and flew off with him, planning to tear him
to bits and eat him piece by piece.

"Oh!" moaned the quail out loud, "how little sense I have! How
stupid I am! This is what I get for leaving my own familiar ground. Oh,
how I wish I had stayed on my own ground. If I had stayed there,
this falcon would have been no match for me!" The quail looked up to
see if the falcon was listening. The falcon was. "Oh, yes," the quail
continued, "had this falcon come to fight me there, I would have
been a match for him."

The falcon roared with laughter. "Where is this place where a
quail can be a match for a falcon?" he asked.

"It is a field, Oh, falcon, plowed and covered with clods of earth."

"An open field!" The falcon laughed so hard he almost dropped
the quail. "Oh, by all means let us fly there, and we shall have our
duel." With a cruel smile, the falcon released the quail.

The quail flew to his field, and the falcon followed behind. When
the quail landed, the falcon cried from high above, "Ready, Oh,
mighty quail?"

The little quail hopped on top of the biggest, hardest clod of

earth he could find and bravely cried,
"Ready, Oh, Falcon."

Straining every nerve and laying
his wings back, the falcon dived.

"Here he comes at top speed,"
thought the quail. He waited until the
falcon was almost upon him. He
could see the large claws and fierce
beak. Then, at the last moment, the
little quail hopped backward off the

clod of earth. The falcon could not stop himself, and he struck the
clod of hard, sun-baked earth at top speed. He died instantly, never
knowing what happened.

The little quail hopped back up on the clod of earth and said:

> The lion in his cave,
> The monkey in his tree,
> The fish in the river,
> And, in the hive, the bee.
>
> The quail in his field,
> And the falcon on the wing:
> On his own ground
> Every one is king.

A Taste of His Own Medicine

Once upon a time, long, long ago, a
big water snake lived in the
river Ganges in a hole beneath a rock.
He used to lie in his hole and wait
for fish to swim by. Whenever one did,
the snake would dart out and catch
the unsuspecting fish and eat it.

One day while swimming around
the river, the snake saw a whole school
of tiny fish feeding together.

"Ah!" he said, "here's a fine lot of fish. I won't have to wait for my supper today." And, so saying, he slipped into the middle of the school of fish with his jaws wide open. But before he could eat a single one, all the fish joined together and began to bite him. They nipped and snapped and bit until he was covered with blood. In fear of his life, the snake swam away and lay down, full of pain, at the edge of the river. He saw there a big green frog who was sunning himself on a flat rock by the river bank. The snake complained to him:

"Sir, does it seem fair to you that all those fish should attack me that way?"

The big green frog blinked his eyes, looked at the snake, and said:

"Why not? You eat fish one by one as they swim by your hole. You thought you could eat them two by two by sneaking into their feeding ground. But you found that in numbers there is strength. You are just like all bullies. You are happy picking on others—until the tables are turned." Then the frog added:

> Snakes eat fish as long as they
> Can get away with it;
> But listen to the biter cry
> The minute he is bit!

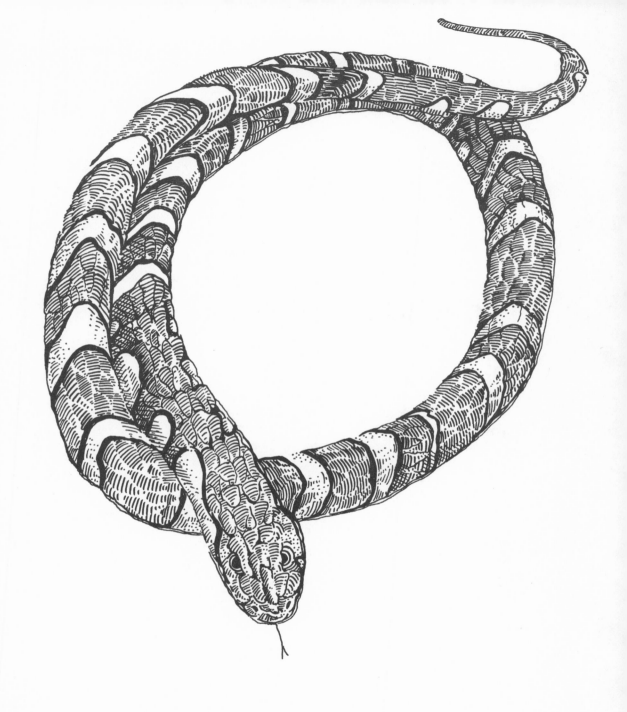

Cooperation

L ong, long ago when Brahmadatta was king of Benares, a hunter of birds used to go to the forest every day to net quail. This hunter could imitate all of a quail's different calls so perfectly that every quail within earshot would fly toward the sound. As soon as they landed and flocked together, he would throw a big net over them. He took the trapped quail home, fattened them, and sold them at.market.

In time, one of the quail called the others together and said, "This hunter is killing off our kinfolk by the dozens. His whistle is so clever that none of us can tell true calls from false calls. But I have a plan to free us from his net. Listen carefully. When he throws the net over us, each of us must stick his head through a hole in the net. Then, all together, we must rise up and fly away quickly, net and all. We must fly until we reach the nearest thorn bush. There, we can land and let the net fall over the thorns. Then we can slip out beneath and make our escape."

"Good!" all the quail agreed.

The very next day they had a chance to try the plan. The hunter came to the woods and sounded a quail call so cleverly that all the quail within earshot thought it came from a member of their own flock, and they quickly gathered together—only to have the net thrown over them.

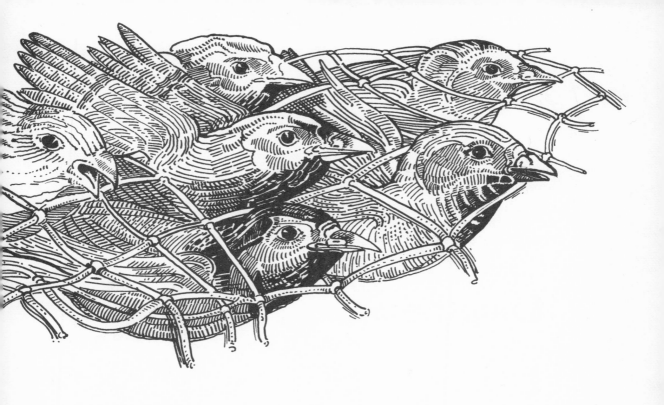

But this time they knew what to do. Each quail stuck its head through a hole in the net; then, together, they rose and flew away, carrying the net with them. When they reached a thorn bush, they landed. The net stuck on the thorns, and the quail dropped beneath the bush and ran away. When evening came, the hunter was still picking his net out of the thorn bush.

The next day and the day after the quail played the same trick. Soon, it became a regular sight to see the hunter picking his net out of thorn bushes as sun set. Day after day he went home empty-handed.

His friends and family grew worried. "What will become of you?" they asked. The hunter replied, "Those quail have begun to cooperate and work together. But," he continued, "don't worry about me. The quail will not always live in such harmony. As soon as they start quarreling among themselves, I will bag the lot of them."

Not long after this, while landing at their feeding ground, one quail by accident stepped on another's head.

"Who stepped on my head?" said the first quail.

"I did," said the second, "but there's no need to start screaming. It was a mistake."

This answer made the first quail angrier than before, and soon the two of them began to trade insults.

Shortly, a third quail joined the argument. "Why be so high and mighty?" he asked. "I suppose you think *you* alone lift up the net?"

"Well, I know it isn't *you*," the first quail answered. "You don't even carry your own share."

And so the birds argued back and forth.

A few days later, the hunter came back to the forest. As usual, he lured the quail together by his call. Then he threw his net over them.

As soon as the net was over them, the third quail said to the first quail, who was near him, "All right, mighty bird, now's your chance to fly away with the net all by yourself."

"Not I!" the quail answered. "I wouldn't want to take away your moment of glory. Lift away yourself, Oh, King of Birds!" And all the quail started to argue. While they were quarreling, the hunter quietly gathered the four corners of the net together and took the quail home singing:

When we forget our common need,
And act instead from selfish greed,
We put ourselves in danger, all:
United we stand; divided we fall!

Decide for Yourself

Once upon a time when Brahmadatta was king of Benares, a jackal named Mayavi and his mate lived by the river bank. By this same river, lived two otters, one named Gambhi and one named Anuti.

One day, the two otters were standing on the river bank looking for fish to catch. Gambhi spotted a great rohita fish; he dove into the water after it and grabbed it by the tail. But the fish was so strong that it swam away, dragging the otter behind.

Gambhi called out, "Friend Anuti, help me! I caught this fish, but he's swimming away with me. He's big enough for both of us to eat. Come help!"

Anuti jumped into the river to help his friend.

The two otters dragged the rohita fish out of the water and laid it on the bank. Said Gambhi to Anuti, "How shall we divide it?"

Said Anuti to Gambhi, "I don't know. *You* divide it."

Gambhi protested, "I don't know where to begin. Why don't *you* divide it?" So the otters just stood there on the river bank, unable to decide who should divide the fish or even how to divide it. They soon were overheard by the jackal, Mayavi. He walked toward them with great dignity.

Seeing the jackal, the two otters saluted him respectfully and said:

"Oh, honored sir, we cannot decide how to divide this fish we caught. Can you solve the problem for us?"

"Oh, yes," Mayavi replied. "I've solved many such problems in my time." Then he said to Gambhi, "You take the head of the fish." The otter did as he was told.

Then the jackal said to Anuti, "You take the tail of the fish." Anuti did so.

"Now," said Mayavi, "I'll take the middle of the fish as payment for my efforts in settling this case." And before the two otters could protest, the jackal made off with the best and biggest part of the fish. The otters were left dumbfounded—one holding only the head and the other only the tail.

When Mayavi's mate saw him coming, she asked him how he came to have such an enormous piece of fish. The jackal told her the story of the two otters who could not come to their own decision. Then he added:

> If for yourself you can't decide,
> Then others will, so don't complain!
> Freedom to choose is easy to loose,
> And once it is lost, hard to regain.

Rumors

Once upon a time when Brahmadatta ruled, a little hare lived near the Western Ocean in a grove of palm and vilva trees. One day, as he was sitting under a vilva tree, the little hare suddenly thought:

"I have heard that sometimes there are earthquakes. The great earth shakes and starts to break into pieces. If an earthquake should start, what would I do?" As he was worrying about this, a ripe vilva fruit fell out of the tree and landed on the ground with a loud THUD!

Jumping up in terror, the hare cried, "Oh, my; Oh, dear; it's happening. The earth is breaking apart!" And he started running toward the ocean.

Another hare saw him rushing off, half frightened to death, and asked what was the matter.

The first hare cried, without stopping, "The earth is breaking apart!" Hearing this, the second hare began to run, too. And so, first one, then another hare joined in until 100,000 hares were all racing toward the ocean.

They were seen by a deer, a boar, an elk, a buffalo, a wild ox, a rhinoceros, a tiger, and an elephant. When these animals, in turn, heard that the earth was breaking apart, they too started to run.

And so, one by one, the number grew and grew until the earth seemed covered with running, terrified animals.

A young lion, who was asleep in his cave high on the hillside, was awakened by the thundering of so many feet. He looked out of his cave and was amazed to see the headlong flight of so many thousands of animals.

"Why," he said, "they are all running toward the ocean. If I don't do something, they will all drown themselves."

So, bounding down from the mountain, the lion ran in front of the stampeding animals and gave the mightiest roar ever heard before or since. The animals, paralyzed with fright, stopped dead in their tracks.

"What is the matter here?" the lion demanded.

"The earth is breaking apart," they cried, all together.

The lion thought, "The earth does not seem to me to be breaking apart," and he began asking questions, starting with the largest animals. "Why are you running?" he asked the elephants.

"The earth is breaking apart," trumpeted the elephants.

"Who saw it breaking apart?" the lion asked.

"The tigers know all about it," the elephants replied.

The tigers said, "The rhinoceroses know."

The rhinoceroses said, "The oxen know."

The oxen said, "The buffaloes know."

The buffaloes said, "The elks know."

The elks said, "The boars."

The boars said, "The deer."

The deer said, "The hares."

When the hares were questioned, they pointed to the little hare and said, "He told us."

The young lion said to the hare, "Is it true, sir, that the earth is breaking apart?"

"Oh, yes, sir," the little hare replied, "I heard it with my own ears!"

"Where?" the lion asked.

"Where I live, sir, a grove of palm and vilva trees. I was lying beneath a vilva tree when I heard the earth start to break apart."

The lion turned to the animals and said, "All of you, wait here. I myself will go to the very spot and see if this is true. Then I will come back and tell you."

Placing the hare on his back, the lion sprang forward with great speed and soon arrived at the palm and vilva grove. "Come," said the lion, "show me the place where the earth is breaking apart."

The hare jumped off his back, not daring to go too near the vilva tree, and pointed. "Over there, sir, is where I heard the awful sound."

The lion went to the place and found the ripe vilva fruit that had fallen to the ground. Picking it up, he said, "Here, sir, is your world breaking apart—no more than a ripe fruit that fell upon the ground."

Then, putting the hare on his back once more, the lion raced back to the frightened herd of animals and said:

"Do not be afraid any longer. You are perfectly safe. The world is not breaking apart. This hare only heard a ripe vilva fruit fall upon the ground." Then he said:

> One foolish creature starts a rumor;
> Ask yourself who is the worst:
> He who takes it for the truth,
> Or he who started it at first?

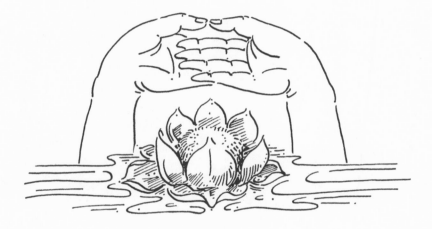

DATE DUE

MAY [4] 78			
AUG 0 '80			
FEB 2 '81			
MAR 2 '82			
MAR 15 '83 APR 10 84			
APR 9 '85			
AUG 6 '85			
Jae			
OC 25 88			
NO 1 88			
NOV 1 6 1989			
FEB 2 8 1992			
GAYLORD			PRINTED IN U.S.A.